S.O.S.

S.O.S.

J. FALLENSTEIN

darbycreek

MINNEAPOLIS

Darby Creek
A division of Lerner Publishing Group, Inc.
241 First Avenue North
Minneapolis, MN 55401 USA

For reading levels and more information, look up this title at www.lernerbooks.com.

Images in this book used with the permission of: © iStockphoto.com/bonciutoma, (ghostly girl); backgrounds: © iStockphoto.com/AF-studio, © iStockphoto.com/blackred, © iStockphoto.com/Adam Smigielski.

Main body text set in Janson Text LT Std 12/17.5.
Typeface provided by Adobe Systems.

Library of Congress Cataloging-in-Publication Data

Names: Fallenstein, J., author.
Title: S.O.S. / J. Fallenstein.
Other titles: SOS
Description: Minneapolis : Darby Creek, [2017] | Series: Midnight | Summary: A teenaged boy who has trouble sleeping stays up late to read, but things take an unexpected turn when weird lights begin to flash S.O.S. through his window.
Identifiers: LCCN 2016028947 (print) | LCCN 2016041028 (ebook) | ISBN 9781512427707 (lb : alk. paper) | ISBN 9781512431001 (pb : alk. paper) | ISBN 9781512427905 (eb pdf)
Subjects: | CYAC: Haunted places—Fiction. | Ghosts—Fiction. | Horror stories.
Classification: LCC PZ7.1.F353 Saam 2017 (print) | LCC PZ7.1.F353 (ebook) | DDC [Fic]—c23

LC record available at https://lccn.loc.gov/2016028947

Manufactured in the United States of America
1-41495-23356-9/6/2016

To my mom, who shared the old family Bible with me—the one that recorded our Swiss and German ancestors in the front. I know who I am a bit better because someone cared and remembered their names, their births, marriages, and deaths.

CHAPTER 1

The frothing, angry waves grow bigger—one foot high, two—then they wash over the front of the kayak.

"Dad!" Tyrell yells over the screaming wind. The sea below swells, and the next wave is like a wall of steel rising up and then crashing down hard, flipping their boat.

Tyrell is under. He gasps, and the cold water rushes into his lungs. Air! He needs air!

He kicks out of the kayak. The icy water penetrates his wet suit to his skin, freezing his muscles.

At last he bobs to the surface and turns on his back, sputtering and coughing out saltwater. "Help!" he yells.

*****

Tyrell sits up. The attic is dark—a dull, late-October twilight. From the corner comes the hum of a small space heater.

"Tyrell?" his mom calls as she hurries up to the top of the narrow stairs, her face pale and drawn.

She sits on his bed, and her hands go to his cheeks. "Another dream?" she says.

Tyrell falls back, and she swipes the back of her hand over his slick forehead.

"It happened again," Tyrell says. "The rogue wave—flipping us. I drowned all over again."

"Shhh," his mom says and squeezes his shoulders. "You're safe now. You and Dad are safe. You didn't drown."

He takes a deep breath. *Why didn't I do something to steady the boat when I saw the wave?* Once they flipped, he didn't check on his dad or try to help him at all. Tyrell has recovered from the hypothermia without permanent injuries, but his dad is another story. "Did they say when he can come home?" he asks.

His mom shakes her head. "No, but he seems better. I think he'll be home this week." She blinks and leans her elbow on the bed, like she wishes she could lie down next to him and sleep. "I'll go and make you some hot tea."

Tyrell glances at the clock. It's just after ten o'clock—he didn't sleep long before the nightmare woke him. His mom leaves, and he looks up and counts the boards in the old cottage's attic. *There are two hundred and fifty-seven. Dad and I were rescued at the same time,* he thinks. *Why did I get to come home after one day in the hospital, but three days later Dad is still there?* He stretches his arms above his head. All of his muscles ache, but the doctor said that should resolve in another day.

The doctor also said she'd seen cases where younger kids suffer no damage from cold-water submersion, but adults . . . well, she'd said it was harder for them to recover. Dad was an experienced kayaker. He'd done three of the five Great Lakes. The weather on the Sound that day was supposed to be calm, but they'd been caught in a sudden storm. They would have been safe, if only they'd been able to make it to Blake Island.

It was a good thing they'd had the beacon. Dad's office friends had made fun of him, told him he wasted three hundred dollars, but that personal locator beacon had saved their lives. The Flauntleroy Ferry was close enough to hear the beacon's signal and rescue them. Good thing those sailors knew what they were doing.

Dishes clink below in the tiny kitchen as his mom gets out the tea things. *It will probably be that awful chamomile.*

His eyes stop on the pile of homework on his desk. The dang civics report is due Friday. *I can't fail another major assignment—there's no way I'm repeating that class!*

"Here we go," his mom says as she brings in a cup of steaming chamomile tea and a bottle of honey. The tea smells and tastes like weeds. He sits up, shivers, and squeezes a huge glob from the honey bear container into his mug.

"When can I see Dad?" He slurps a bit of the abominable liquid.

His mom gives him a weak smile. "Maybe tomorrow. We'll see how you're feeling. Looks like we'll have snow by Halloween," she says, gesturing out the window, which is thick and wavy with age. "Try to get some sleep." She tucks in the thick down comforter along the edge of his bed and then pads back down the creaky steps. A few minutes later the light at the base of the steps goes out and his room is dark. The white moon shines in the window, and Tyrell counts the boards above him again: *two hundred fifty-six, two hundred fifty-seven* . . .

He slips out of bed and stands at the window, breathing a circle of fog onto the glass. The moonlight shimmers on the slate roof tiles of the Schneider mansion, which sits about a quarter mile down the incline and straight ahead. To the right is the acre of old woods that lines the peninsula they live on. Far to the left are two more cottages, empty now, but soon they too will be sold and people will move in. Tiny crystalline snowflakes dance down from the deep lavender sky. He can just make out the narrow lane and then the dark line of the footbridge across the creek that runs behind the mansion. Beyond, at the very tip of the peninsula, sits the old Schneider Wearables Factory, which has been abandoned for decades.

Tyrell's back spasms, and he shifts his weight. A loose board below his foot moans and creaks.

His head is aching, probably because he's been in bed all day. He sits at the old writing desk in the corner and opens his civics book. He just needs to read the chapter on workers' rights and write a simple report. A folded test flutters to the floor from the back of the book, and the red F glares at him. *Dang. I can bring my grade up if I finish the extra credit, but if Mom sees this I'm toast. I have to get rid of it. But where?*

Maybe he can shove the test under that creaky floorboard. It came loose when his mom and dad took the thin 1940s carpet out last week, and when they re-carpet, it will be entombed forever. He crouches at the board, slips his finger underneath, and tugs. The foot-long plank comes up.

In the glow of the moon he can just make out something folded at the bottom of the space underneath—a sheet of yellowed paper. As he unfolds it a ten-dollar bill flutters to the floor. *Ten bucks!* He jabs the bill into his sweats pocket. The top of the page is printed with the red Schneider Wearables company logo, and scratchy cursive writing in blotchy, black ink covers the page. But the language is not English. The date in the corner is smudged, as if a drop of water has fallen on it. It reads "14 Sept 19 . . . " He can't read the year. *Who would have hidden a letter and money under the floorboard and then not come back for it?*

CHAPTER 2

It's past eleven, but Tyrell's still not tired. He clicks on the desk lamp and reads the civics chapter about how in the eighteenth century most goods, cloth, and clothing were created in rural homes, in "cottage industries." But with the invention of new weaving and sewing machinery, cities needed workers to run them. It was most often the poor, newly arrived immigrants who took these low-paying jobs.

He pulls out his laptop and types up an outline, and then he adds a few sentences after each point. Soon he has three pages full of information. It would be so much easier if the teacher just let the class use Wikipedia, but it doesn't matter anyway because this little cottage his parents are fixing up doesn't have Wi-Fi yet. He'll just have to go to the Middleton High library. *Good thing Ms. Lingard is always cool with helping me out. Then again, she's the librarian, so I guess that's what she does.*

He unfolds the old letter. *Liebe Mutter*, it starts. What language is it? German, maybe? The end says, *Deine, Helga.*

He can't show Mom; she will ask where he found it, and he needs that test to stay hidden. *Maybe Ms. L can tell me—that is, if Mom ever lets me go back to school.* He stands and stretches, still achy, and then shivers when the space heater shuts off. The doctor told him not to get cold again or he would end up back in the hospital. But his mom only wants him to run the heater while he's awake—she's worried that it might start a fire while he's asleep.

He yawns, finally tired. It's warm under all the blankets his mom piled on the bed. Maybe now he can sleep and not have the drowning dream.

Just as Tyrell shuts off his desk lamp, something out the window catches his eye.

A light, yellow and small, flashes from somewhere beyond the mansion. He presses his face to the cold glass as the light pulses again. *Flash-flash-flash, flaaasssh-flaaasssh-flaaasssh, flash-flash-flash.* It's coming from the top floor of the abandoned warehouse.

A draft jolts a shiver through his body, and he quickly gets under the warm down comforter. Who would be up in the third story of that old warehouse at midnight? Is there a wire loose somewhere? Or is the light flashing at him?

CHAPTER 3

Tyrell wakes to the greasy, savory smell of his mom frying eggs in the kitchen. His muscles ache less, so he dresses and packs his backpack, folding the old letter into the side pocket.

"Morning," he says as he walks into the kitchen and sets his backpack on the floor. Mom eyes it.

"Tyrell," she says, "you don't think you're going to school, do you?"

"I feel fine."

"Is that why you slept until eleven?" She slips the eggs onto a plate.

His eyes shoot to the microwave: 11:14. "You're kidding me."

Mom shakes her head and raises her eyebrows. "I don't think you're quite there. Besides, it's already Friday and halfway through the school day. Let's wait until Monday to send you back."

Tyrell sighs and picks up his fork. The eggs are warm and buttery. "I have a report due and . . . " He can't tell her that he failed the test. "I need books for it. It's important."

"I can take you to school, and you can pick up your books while I run to the hardware store and order the carpet for your room."

It's not what he wanted, but it's better than staring at the ceiling for another whole day. Plus, once that new carpet is laid down that old test will be hidden forever. "Okay, Mom."

*****

At school there is more homework than Tyrell was expecting, especially in chemistry. His mom texts, *There in 20.* Twenty minutes. He heads for the library.

"Tyrell," Ms. Lingard says when he comes through the door.

"How you doing, Ms. L?"

"I'm doing well, thank you. It's good to see you. I heard about your accident. Everybody okay?"

"Dad's still in the hospital, but they think he can come home soon."

"It was bad?"

"I guess. I mean, I almost died. The worst part is Mom. She's just . . . you know, worried."

"I'm so glad you guys are okay. You're holding up all right?"

"I do have a ton of homework, including this report on the Triangle Shirtwaist Factory fire," Tyrell says.

"Oh, civics," Ms. L says. "You're on the workers' rights chapter, I take it?"

Tyrell nods. "I need primary, academic, and news sources to quote for my paper."

"I have just the book!" She walks over to one of the shelves and returns with a book called *The Last Stitch*. "It's about the Shirtwaist fire. It's got all kinds of information on child labor and the garment workers. Perfect for your report," she says. "And did you say you wanted some copies of old newspaper articles?" She winks her eye conspiratorially.

"Yes, ma'am, I did."

She steps into her office and returns with a manila file folder. "I wouldn't do this for everyone, but I already made copies for your teacher, and you've been out on an illness, so . . . " She hands him the folder.

"Ms. L, you are awesome," he says. "Always got my back."

"It's my job. The fact is, you come in and ask for help, and not all students take the time to do that," Ms. L says. "Anything else?"

He unzips the backpack pocket and pulls out the letter. "I found this up in my attic, and I'm wondering if you know what language it is."

Her eyes widen as she unfolds the yellowed paper. "*Liebe Mutter*," she reads aloud. "It's definitely German. I haven't spoken German since high school, but I know that means 'Dear Mother.'" She scans the letter. "I think it says something about work, and *der Chef ist böse*

14

translates to 'the boss is mean.' Huh. This was in your attic?"

"Yeah, we live in one of those old cottages on the Schneider estate. My parents bought one last year and we moved there to remodel it."

"Oh, yes, I heard that old Miss Schneider was finally selling the outbuildings. Good thing—they were likely to fall apart if somebody didn't get in and restore them. Miss Schneider, now, she's an odd duck."

"Yeah, I heard Sean say that she's crazy— she lives all alone and wears her old wedding dress every day, even though the guy she was supposed to marry died, like, a million years ago. Did she kill him or something?"

"No, she didn't—I hadn't heard that rumor before! She's the daughter of Max Schneider, the man who started Schneider Wearables back in 1918 or so. He became a multimillionaire. She was supposed to get married when she was seventeen, but her fiancé died in a hunting accident. She still runs the business, but people say she never got over him."

Tyrell hoists his backpack. This is interesting—kinda spooky, even—but his mom is probably already out front, honking the horn. "Well, I gotta go," he says. "Thanks for helping me out."

"You're welcome!" Ms. L holds up the letter. "Give me a day or two, and I'll get this translated. Will you be back Monday?"

"If I have any luck at all."

"You keep working on that report, and I'll see you then."

His phone buzzes in his pocket as he goes out the library door; his mom must be out front. *Shoot*, he thinks, *the name on the bottom of the letter is Helga. I should have asked if that's Miss Schneider's name. And what was that light coming from the factory? Is Miss Schneider doing something over there, since she owns the place? I'll stay up tonight and watch.*

CHAPTER 4

"New Schneider Wearables Factory to Be Built" reads the headline in a 1917 article from the folder. The article describes the new factory as surrounded by water and therefore impervious to fire. But then the next copied article says that in 1928 the Schneider Wearables Factory did catch fire. He snorts. It was just a small fire on the third floor, though, and nobody died.

Tyrell's headache is almost gone, probably because he is out of bed for a change. It's cold and dark, and the attic grows chillier the later it gets. His reflection in the window looks almost like a ghost, gaunt and pale. The doctor had said his skin was blue-gray when he'd first been admitted. He is still pale but definitely not blue. The small space heater clicks off. Mom said to unplug it before he went to sleep. "We don't need the place to go up in flames," she always warned.

She is even more vigilant since the kayak accident, always telling him to stay warm, feeding him hot meals and terrible tea, and not letting him out of her sight. *And she seemed . . . was it angry?* he wonders. *Angry with Dad?*

Had Dad been reckless, taking Tyrell out on the Sound when the forecast called for light rain? He'd said something about a bad wind from the south—was it a premonition? Before they launched, Dad had even hastily shown Tyrell how to use a mirror to send the distress signal S.O.S.: three quick flashes, three long ones, and three quick ones. Dad had never done that before a kayak ride.

The lights in the kitchen are off now. *Mom must be in bed, asleep. She's finally not staying up all night, checking on me!* Tyrell takes out the book from Ms. L and reads a chapter on the Triangle Shirtwaist Factory fire. It happened in

1911, when the clothing factory caught fire and 145 people died. Most of the casualties were poor, young women. Many of them died after jumping out of the windows to escape. They couldn't get out because someone had locked the workers in—supposedly to prevent stealing. There was a fire escape, but it was tiny and in disrepair, and the one working elevator was small and slow and couldn't accommodate all of the workers. It was a disaster.

At a quarter to midnight Tyrell clicks off the desk lamp. His head throbs, but he can't take another night of staring at the ceiling. He puts his pillow at the other end of the bed so that he can look out at the Schneider mansion, the creek, and the moonlight. His eyes are heavy. He is just drifting off when something—a gentle burst of light—wakes him. *The flashes!* He sits up and moves to the window. *Yes, the flashes are coming from the building's third story. Who is up there?*

The flashes are in the same pattern Tyrell's dad showed him, the international code for S.O.S. Tyrell strains his aching eyes and watches.

Who could possibly be up there in the burned-out factory, sending a signal? And to whom? There aren't any businesses or coast guard stations on that side, only the Schneider mansion and a few cottages. And only his cottage is occupied. Is the message meant for him?

CHAPTER 5

On Sunday, at the hospital, Tyrell and his mom push through the swinging metal doors and turn left into a sterile-smelling room.

"Hey, Champ!" Dad's voice is gravelly, and his good mood seems forced. He's sitting up, wearing a light blue and white hospital gown. He coughs and lets out a long, rough breath. A plastic IV tube runs over the top of his hand and connects to an IV bag on a hook.

Dad has barely any color in his cheeks, and he looks more tired than Tyrell has ever seen him. But he is alive.

"They say I can go home tomorrow," his dad says.

"Really?" Tyrell can't help but look at the IV bag.

His dad smiles, trying to look reassuring. "I'll be back to normal real soon now." The crinkles around his eyes seem deeper, older. "You're all better, Ty?"

"Yeah. I'm fine, Dad." Tyrell manages a smile. He didn't have the drowning dream last night, so maybe it was true.

Mom kisses Dad's head and sits in the chair. "Once *you're* all better we can finish the attic. Ty can't sleep up there anymore if it's not insulated."

The nurse walks in. "Sorry, folks," he says, "but we need to take him down the hall to run a couple of tests now."

"That was a short visit," his mom says brusquely. But the nurse stands his ground, and Mom stands up. "Okay, Ty, I'll drop you at home and then grab some groceries." She puts on her we-can-do-it face and says, "We'll have Dad's favorite meal tomorrow."

"That's right," his dad says hoarsely. "I'll be

there." But his smile is weak, and his eyes don't look so sure.

*****

A light mist coats the windshield as they drive down the winding gravel road and pull into the driveway.

"I'll be back in a half hour or so," his mom says as Tyrell unbuckles his seat belt. "Stay in the cottage: the last thing we need is for you to get a chill."

He hurries inside as her car pulls away, but he turns to the window to look down at the factory. *I saw it last night too. Was it just a short in the wiring, or is someone really sending an S.O.S.? It would only take me ten minutes to bike down to the factory,* he muses. *I could check out the building and see if someone is in there—if they need help. I could save someone, just like the ferry crew saved me and Dad. Pay it back.*

I'll dress warmly, he promises himself. *Besides, I'm going stir-crazy staying home all the time.*

Wrapped in several layers, he backs his bike out of the shed, careful not to snag any of the garden tools or bump into the old lawnmower. His scarf snags on the old iron key ring hanging by the door, and the ring slips off the nail. He catches it and hangs it up again. It's kind of cool, full of weird old keys—he found it when his mom told him to hide a spare key to the cottage somewhere and he picked the shed.

Tyrell shrugs deeper into his jacket as he coasts down the narrow lane. The wind whistles in his ears. They sting with cold. As he rides by the mansion, he glances at the yellow satin drapes that are pulled almost shut all along the mansion's main-floor windows. *Is Miss Schneider really in there in her wedding dress?*

He stops at the end of the lane, a foot before the century-old footbridge that crosses the creek. It's only about four bike lengths across, but it's not much wider than the span of his arms, and some of the boards are cracked. *You'd never get a car across this*, he thinks. *It must have been the bridge that the Schneider workers used to get to work at the factory. Is it still safe?*

Tentatively he rolls forward. The gray boards wobble and creak. *Well, if I fall in, the stream is only a few feet down and it isn't that deep. But it will be cold, and I can't afford to get cold again.*

At last Tyrell bumps over the bridge's metal threshold and rides slowly up to the three-story factory. It is a rectangle, long and narrow. All of the windows are boarded up except for one in the corner of the third floor: that's where the flashing light comes from. The letters molded deep into the concrete block above the oversized front entrance read *Schneider Wearables 1917*. The black iron handles of the huge wooden doors are chained and padlocked.

There must be a way in somewhere—someone was definitely signaling from the third floor. He rides around the perimeter of the building. The basement windows are all barred, and the smaller windows on the second floor in the back are boarded over as well—except for one. It is in the back, facing the bay. A big, gray metal pipe with smaller pipes branching from it runs up the wall nearby.

Tyrell rides back to the front, dismounts and parks his bike, and then stands below the open third-floor window. "Hello?" he calls. He looks up at the gray sky and then at the window. Icy raindrops dampen his face and cloud his vision. *I should go home. I don't want to end up in the hospital just as Dad gets out. But what if nobody had helped us just because it was cold and wet on the Sound? We would have died. I have to try.*

"Is anybody there?" he shouts.

No one calls back. He cups his hands around his mouth. "Do you need help? Talk to me."

The wind carries his voice out to the bay, where it is absorbed by the sound of waves crashing on the rocky embankment.

"Hello? Let me see you so I can help you."

He glances back at the Schneider mansion. The yellow curtains sway. Is someone watching him?

Beyond the mansion he sees his family's small wood and stone cabin. *If Mom comes back and finds me gone, she will freak and I won't be allowed outside for a week.* He heads home through the light rain. But when he looks back at the factory, a shadow shifts behind the window, as if someone has just walked by.

CHAPTER 6

Tyrell has just walked through the door and taken off his wet jacket when Mom's car pulls up the slight hill near the shed. *Mom will definitely notice that my jacket is wet. There's only one way to hide the evidence.*

He throws the jacket on again and rushes out to the car, calling, "I'll help you." He grabs the two paper bags of groceries and runs back into the cottage.

"What's on your agenda today?" Mom asks once the groceries are put away. He can tell that she's worried about his dad but is trying to hide it. But she's pacing, which is a dead giveaway.

"I've got that civics paper due," he says.

"The one on workers' rights." He heads for the narrow attic stairs.

"Turn on the space heater, but remember to unplug it when you're done," his mom says.

Tyrell pages through the newspaper copies Ms. L gave him about the fire in the Schneider Wearables Factory. Many German and Irish immigrants worked there. Some writers claimed that building was a sweatshop, a place where poor people worked nearly as slaves making garments. He skims the article:

BELLEVUE, Sept. 14 – Fire of unknown origin partially destroyed the third floor of the Schneider Wearables Factory in Middleton Friday night. The materials and sewing machines are a total loss.

The factory is owned by Max Schneider of Middleton and managed by Herbert Zinn of Seattle. A general alarm was sent out to which all fire departments in the city responded, but the fire had been extinguished by Zinn and two other workers by the time firefighters arrived. Zinn said no workers were in the building during the fire and no one was injured. It is not known when the factory will reopen, but Zinn said operations will be moved to a new building nearer the city and away from the Schneider estate, which was spared from the fire.

Weird, Tyrell thinks. *If only part of the third floor was damaged, why would they move the whole factory downtown? It's like the manager wanted to get out of the Schneider factory as fast as possible. Maybe he wanted it closer to his home or something.*

Tyrell closes the file. If no one died, and if he can't prove that it was a sweatshop, then the Schneider fire will not work for his paper on workers' rights. Too bad, because with the factory so close it would have been interesting to interview Miss Schneider, if she would let him, about the company and her father. Plus, then he'd find out if Miss Schneider really did roam the mansion in her wedding dress.

The Triangle Shirtwaist Factory fire will just have to be the focus of his paper. *But I won't get extra credit unless I come up with a second example of a workers' rights violation. What can I do?*

Just after eight o'clock he finishes a rough draft and takes his laptop down to the tiny kitchen for his mom to proofread it. Mixing bowls are out, and a sweet, warm scent wafts from the oven. Dozens of cupcakes, a chocolate cake, and two pies sit on the counter. *Mom must be distracting herself from worrying about Dad.* She hands him a broken cupcake, and says, "Can't let the ugly ones go to waste!" before she reads his paper.

The rich chocolate cupcake is still hot and totally delicious, but the flashing light in the factory won't leave his mind. Is someone up there?

"Mom—" he starts.

"Hmmm?" She doesn't look up from his laptop.

If there is someone trapped in the factory, why didn't they call out to him? Are they hurt? Tied up by some kidnapper?

He has to tell her. "I think there's someone . . . "

"Yes?" she says distractedly. "Someone what?" She glances up at him.

But what if it's just a short in the wiring? She'll call the rescue workers and they'll find nothing, and everyone will look at me like I'm crazy.

"Someone who could really use a cupcake," he recovers quickly. "Can I take a couple to school?"

"Sure, Ty." She goes back to his paper.

I'll watch and see if it happens again. If it flashes S.O.S., I'll tell Mom and we can check it out. He finishes the cupcake and after a few minutes grabs another one.

"Looks pretty good," his mom says, turning his laptop to him. "You've got a couple grammatical errors, and you repeat this part about how the immigrants were undocumented and didn't speak English. And the jumping to their deaths is mentioned, I think, four times— might be overkill. Wow. That fire sounds terrible." She bites her lip and manages a smile. "And it looks like you're not quite done."

"Yeah," Tyrell says. *Maybe she's thinking again about how I almost died.* He tries to comfort her, saying, "They were really helpless, taken advantage of. But the good thing is that after that fire there were many more laws to protect people like them." He yawns, closes the computer, and gets up.

"Going to bed?" Mom motions for him to wipe the corners of his mouth.

"Yeah." He licks away the chocolate. "But I set my alarm to wake me up so I can finish this paper."

"When is it due?"

"Friday."

"Good boy. I'll just wait for this last cake and head to bed too.

Upstairs, Tyrell lies down on his bed and sets the alarm. The space heater hums, and it is warm under the thick down comforter. He double-checks his alarm. He will wake just before midnight and watch for the light.

His eyes do not want to stay open, and he pulls the pillow over his forehead as another raging headache starts. After what feels like ages, his muscles unclench and he sinks into the bed.

Then someone is in his room, watching him. He tries to open his eyes, but they are stuck shut. Something heavy is on his chest, pinning him to the mattress. He tries to call out, but no sound comes out except a breathy gasp. Through the tiny slits in his eyes he peers out from under the pillow.

A tentacle of moonlight unfurls like smoke through his window, and suddenly a girl, maybe fourteen or fifteen years old, appears at his desk, writing a letter. Her hair is up in a big, loose bun, and her shirt is white with a tall collar. She is in a long skirt. She turns to him.

"Who— Who are you?" he manages to whisper.

"*Hilf mir,*" she says, her sad eyes pleading. "*Hilf mir.*"

"What?"

"*Ofen,*" she says.

"I don't understand." Tyrell focuses on his legs, telling them to move and get out of bed, but they do not respond. She lifts her arm and points out the window.

"*Ofen,*" she says again.

*****

"Tyrell." His mom shakes his shoulder. "Time to get up."

He sits up, and the pillow falls to the floor. The attic is full of daylight. The girl is gone.

"Where'd she go?" Tyrell rubs his face and looks about the room.

"Who?"

"That girl. She was here, at the desk."

"Wow. Sounds like quite a dream. You must have slept deeply."

"Mom, why are you up here?"

"Didn't you say you wanted to go back to school today?" She smiles.

He turns to the window. He missed the signal. "My alarm." He reaches for the clock.

"Oh, I came up here to turn off the space heater after I took the cake out of the oven, and you were so sound asleep I turned it off."

"But Mom—"

"The doctor said you needed rest. Since the nightmares have finally subsided, I thought it was best to let you sleep." She looks confused. "Why are you so worried about that paper? It's not due until Friday, right?"

35

"Yeah." Slowly he gets out of bed. The desk is just as he left it, with his computer and civics book. But the room is chilly, like the window was open and a cold draft came in.

"Brrr," his mom says and rubs her arms. "Get dressed and I'll drive you to school." She heads to the stairs. "I'm sure you've been bored silly here at home."

He glances out the window, past the Schneider mansion to the factory. Who is up there?

*****

"Hello, Ty," Ms. L says as he walks into the library. "How's the paper coming?"

"Good. Thanks for the book. It was super helpful."

"Oh, I'm glad. How's the remodeling going? Catch any sightings of Miss Schneider?"

"No. But what else do you know about the Schneider Wearables Factory?"

"Well, let's check the database." She motions for him to follow her into her office.

They find a couple of old stories, including

one announcing the hiring of Mr. Zinn, the new factory manager. In a black-and-white photo next to the article, Max Schneider is handing over a large ring of antique keys to Mr. Zinn. The key ring is just like the set that hangs in the shed.

Are they the keys to the factory? If they are, it would be easy to get inside.

Should I tell Ms. L about the signal that comes at midnight from the old building?

No. Because she might tell Mom, and Mom is already so worried about Dad that she's doing crazy things like baking a month's worth of cakes at night. And if Dad is really coming home, she'll have enough on her hands caring for him.

"Oh, look," Ms. L says, pointing to her screen. "Back in the 1970s people used to boat to the peninsula and hang out by the old factory. It looks like something strange happened."

"What?" Tyrell leans over to look.

"Some kids started saying the place was haunted, that they'd been chased out by a madwoman with a pair of scissors."

A chill creeps up his spine.

Ms. L grabs her folder of copies and pulls one out. "Here's an article from last week, some city council notes. Oh, Ty!" She points to a line in the text. "It says that the old factory is slated for demolition *next week*."

"But what if there is . . . " He stops. *No. I can't tell Ms. L.* He forces a smile. "A madwoman with scissors? Ha."

"Ha is right!" She slaps the desk. "The things kids will tell police so they don't get into trouble for trespassing."

Trespassing. The person up in the factory is trespassing. But is it still trespassing if you live on the property and have a key? I will find out. Tonight.

CHAPTER 7

After school, as they pull up the drive,
Mom's phone rings. Tyrell gets out of the
car and steps into the shed. The old key
ring is still on the nail just inside the door.
He takes a closer look: there are four big,
antique keys and two smaller keys on it. One
small key has a hollow barrel, maybe for
a padlock.

"Tyrell?" Mom calls from the car.

It's a big ring, and he can't quite fit it into
his pocket.

"They said Dad can come home today!"
Mom says excitedly from the car. "I'm leaving
now to get him." She beams. "Do you want to
come along?"

"No, I'll wait here," Tyrell says. "With the baked goods. To protect them." He gives the ring a hard shove, and it slides into the pocket.

"Protect them?" Mom questions, "From what?"

"From someone else eating them," he says.

"Okay," Mom says with a real smile. "Stay put." She gives him a wink and drives off.

When Dad walks through the cottage's small front door he looks like a zombie, with dark circles under his eyes, gray skin, and stiff, unnatural movements.

Tyrell holds the door and reaches out to help, but Dad shakes him off. "I can do it," Dad says. Tyrell's stomach sinks. *It's as if Dad doesn't trust me. Does he think I failed him, that day in the water?* Tyrell's eyes fill with hot tears. *If only I could have reached Dad, gotten him out of the water and back onto the kayak, then he wouldn't have gotten hypothermia, wouldn't have had to go the hospital. But instead I came out okay, and Dad might have permanent damage.*

I have to do something—anything—to show Dad that I'm not useless.

"I have a surprise for you," Mom says from the kitchen. She uncovers the frosted carrot cake and then waves a hand over the cupcakes and pies on the table behind her.

"Man, it feels good to be home." Dad sits at the small table.

As they eat, his dad talks haltingly about the strange dreams he had in the hospital. "There was a fire—but on the kayak. Must have been a side effect from the medicine," he says. He smiles weakly at Tyrell, but it isn't like it used to be. It's like he's disappointed.

Tyrell avoids Dad's gaze and gulps down his milk. His dreams have been weird too, but he isn't taking any medicine.

His mom makes the awful chamomile tea, and they sit in the kitchen, listening to the wind howl through the old stone walls of the cottage. "Once I get my energy back we'll finish that attic," his dad says, brushing crumbs from his shirt. He nods at Tyrell.

"Tyrell, maybe you should sleep down here on the couch tonight," his mom says.

"Um." Tyrell glances at the couch. "I don't

think I need to, Mom." *If I stay downstairs, I won't be able to see the signal.*

"We just can't have you getting cold," his mom warns. "It's going to get down to freezing."

"But it's not cold up there," Tyrell insists.

His dad sits up. "If we leave the door open at the bottom of the stairs, the heat should get upstairs," he says.

"Great!" Tyrell hops up before his mom can intervene. "Glad you're home, Dad. I gotta get some homework done before bed." He heads up the narrow stairs.

Downstairs the TV plays and then the dishes clink in the sink as his mom washes them. *If Dad doesn't get better—all better—I'll never be able to look him in the eye again.*

Just after eleven o'clock the light snaps off at the bottom of the steps. Tyrell lies on his bed, propped up so he can see the factory, and waits. At exactly midnight the yellow light throbs: three short, three long, and three short. *Someone has to be up there. A short in the wiring would just make a random flash.*

Silently, Tyrell gets into his snow pants and jacket. *I have the keys, so I can get up there and find out who's inside. It won't take long. And if I don't go now, the person could freeze to death, and then Dad won't be the only one hurt because I didn't do anything.* He puts a small flashlight into his coat pocket, where it clinks against the key ring.

Slowly he opens the creaking shed door and rolls his bike back. As he glides down the lane, a glow comes from behind the parted curtains on the main floor of the Schneider mansion. Someone is in there, watching.

He pedals through the weeds, his heart racing. Is it Miss Schneider?

The blustery wind chafes his cheeks and howls through the warped and cracked boards of the narrow footbridge. A snowstorm is coming. He tucks his head as he rumbles over the creek.

Tiny snowflakes hit his face like pinpricks as he parks his bike and walks up to the front doors. He tugs the key ring from his pocket and tries each key.

None of the keys fit. He drops the lock, and it clangs against the iron handle. The signal glows above.

He steps back. "Hey!" he calls. "Who's up there? It's gonna freeze tonight—let me help you!"

The light flashes again. He has to get to them before it's too late.

"Hey!" Tyrell shouts as he runs to the back of the building. Before he knows it, he is climbing the big gray pipe. He kicks the rest of the glass out of the second-floor window frame and balances for a second before lunging into the dark building.

He takes out the flashlight and turns it on. The room is large and empty except for some litter and old beer bottles. *Probably from those trespassers from the 1970s*, he thinks. In the corner, an old wooden chair sits next to a dusty metal file cabinet. The entire room is lined with shelves, empty except for cobwebs.

In another corner a metal staircase hangs precariously from the ceiling. The bottom half of the steps is missing, as if the staircase was ripped apart. There's no way to get up there.

"Hello? Do you need help?" he yells up the broken staircase. No answer. He has to get up to the third floor, to where the 1928 fire was.

CHAPTER 8

The heavy file cabinet screeches as Tyrell moves it under the stairs. He steps up on top of it, but the staircase's bottom step and scrolled metal railing are still inches above his reach. He gets down and sets the chair on top of the cabinet. The legs fit over the top, but just barely. If the chair tips he could easily fall.

Carefully he steps onto the cabinet and then the wobbly chair seat. His hands grip the cold, wrought-iron railing of the staircase, and he pulls himself up onto the steps. The metal whines and creaks as he takes one step, then another, then another, until finally he is on the wooden planks of the third floor.

The thin flashlight beam reveals a room with two long tables. A broken chair lies near a big, black wood-burning stove with a corroded copper stovepipe. The room smells faintly of smoke. At the far end of the room is a warped wooden door covered with peeling green paint.

If the fire only partially destroyed the third floor, then that door must lead to where the fire was. Its edges glow with yellow light as the signal flashes. *Someone is in there!*

Tyrell's shoes crunch over decades of grit and dust as he slowly approaches the door.

"Hello?" he calls tentatively. "I'm here to help you." The wind howls through the roof slates. Something skitters in the rafters above. A sick feeling fills him. *Something happened here. Something isn't right.*

He grabs the metal doorknob. "Who's there?" he asks as he turns the knob. But it's locked. He pulls the iron key ring from his pocket. The keys jingle as he tries the first antique key. It slides in, and when he turns it the door opens.

The room is barely bigger than a bathroom. A charred smell fills his nose as he peers in from the doorway, and he sneezes. The corner and far wall are burned black; near the wall some of the planks of the wood floor are burned all the way through.

"Hello?" he calls again, his voice barely a whisper. The room is empty, but he feels a presence, as if someone were just here or is still here, hiding.

But how? The room was locked from the outside. The single window is sooty and black; the discolored paint on the metal bars over it has cracked and bubbled with heat. An old sewing machine and a lamp, both scorched, sit on a blackened metal desk. The lamp's bulb flashes the code for S.O.S.

Is it just a short?

This is definitely the room that burned in 1928. Tyrell steps inside, onto a charred floor beam. The door creaks closed behind him, and he spins. The back of the door is splintered and scratched with deep gouges, as if someone attacked it with a knife.

"Hey!" He pulls the door back open, but no one is there. Something chitters in the darkness. The door creaks on its hinges.

"Who's here?" he calls over the sound of his pounding heart.

Whooooo, the wind echoes.

The hairs on his neck rise. Someone is in the factory—watching, waiting. He can sense their eyes watching him and practically feel their breath.

"Show yourself." He turns to face the small burned-out room, shining his flashlight into each of the corners.

The switch on the light moves, and the bulb flashes before going dark. His eyes stop on an old domed chest on the floor. It is locked with a small brass padlock. It is the only thing in the room that is not charred.

"Who are you?" Tyrell whispers.

The light goes on, and the reflection of a young woman—the same girl who was in his room—appears in the window. She is sitting at the desk, sewing by candlelight. Behind her stands a man whose face is menacing and angry but somehow familiar.

The man lifts a key. That reflection fades as the lamp goes out, and when it flashes again an orange glow has appeared in a barrel behind the girl. With each flash of the bulb, the flames grow.

When the light flashes again, it shows the girl at the door, pounding on it. The light goes out and the reflection vanishes.

"What do you want?" he cries out to the empty room.

But only the moaning wind answers in the dark: *Fair shh loss ennn*. In the next flash the girl is standing, her eyes wide and wild. The scissors glint in the orange, flickering light of flames as she turns to Tyrell and raises them.

The woman with the scissors!

Tyrell lunges for the door, but his foot slips off the charred beam and he falls between the floorboards. He grunts with pain as he catches the beam on his way down. His flashlight rolls across the boards and stops next to the chest.

Reeling, he sucks in some air. "Help!" he groans, kicking his legs, trying to pull himself back up.

He still grips the iron key ring, but his hands are slick.

A wail rises from the deep within the corner blackness, and as it crescendos it sounds like a young girl crying, crying.

His fingers slip from the wood, and he drops into the darkness below.

CHAPTER 9

Tyrell's ankle screams in pain when he hits the floor below, and the key ring jingles somewhere in the blackness as it crashes to the ground. He glances up at the hole in the ceiling. *Is she still there? Will she come after me?*

Tyrell stands and limps past the stacked cabinet and chair to the open, moonlit window. He slides down the pipe to the ground and bolts around the building—right into a police officer.

"Got him!" the officer shouts. She grabs his coat and pulls him to the front of the factory. He squints in the light that glares from the squad car parked across the footbridge at the end of the narrow lane.

"Legs apart," she says as she pats him down.

"Tyrell?" His mom hurries down the lane past the squad car. The bottom of her red nightgown drags along the snow-dusted boards of the footbridge. She stops, open-mouthed, a few steps from him.

"Anyone else up there with you?" the officer asks Tyrell as she lets go of his coat.

His jaw clamps shut at her question.

"Well?" the officer asks, crossing her arms.

"Ah—I mean, no. Just me," he says.

"One perp, unarmed, simple trespassing," the officer says into her small shoulder radio. She nods and waves to her partner in the squad car.

"What were you doing?" his mom questions.

"Vandalism?" the officer pushes.

"No." Tyrell can't stop trembling, and his voice shakes. "I was just up on the third floor." He points to the window.

The partner gets out of the squad car. "I'll secure the premises," he says. He looks like a football player. He strides to the front doors of the factory, opens the padlock with a key, and then turns on a huge black flashlight as he goes in.

The first officer turns and looks Tyrell in the eye. "So why were you up there?" She stands almost at attention in her blue uniform as she writes in a small white notebook.

"It's hard to explain," Tyrell says. A shiver shakes him as the image of the woman with the scissors flashes in his mind. "But that light—" He motions to the third-floor window where the yellow light came from. But the window is dark.

"You saw a light?" the officer asks.

"Yes." Tyrell's jaw is shaking and it's hard to form the words. "There was an S.O.S. signal. It came from up there. I went to check it out."

"Oh, Ty." His mom looks as if she's going to cry. "He just got over hypothermia," she explains weakly to the officer. "He's been having these ideas." Her eyes fill with tears. "We thought he was okay, but maybe there was some cognitive damage."

"Mom, I'm not hallucinating," Tyrell insists. His heart pounds, and his voice catches in his throat. He turns back to the window, but it's still dark. "I know what I saw. There's a girl up there. She has these scissors and she's trying to—"

"Oh no." The officer rolls her eyes and holds up her hand. "Not that old story again."

"She's there," Tyrell cries. "I saw her reflection."

The officer's pen stops.

"Her reflection?" his mom asks.

He nods. "There was a fire. At first she was trying to get out. And then she turned."

"All clear," the other officer's voice comes through the radio.

"Tyrell, I think this civics report has really gotten to you," his mom says.

"But I saw her!"

His mom puts her arm around his shoulder and pulls him close. "I know you think you saw someone, but the officer just said there's no one up there."

"Maybe it's her ghost then," Tyrell practically shouts. "I saw her!"

The shoulder radio emits a burst of static, and then the man's voice comes through. "Looks like he climbed on a desk and chair to get up to the third floor."

"Any vandalism?" the first officer asks into the small radio.

"Not that I can tell," comes the reply.

A light comes on at the back of the Schneider mansion, and a door opens. A petite woman in a long white gown emerges. The snow swirls around her as she walks haltingly across the snow-covered lawn toward them. She appears to be floating.

"What in tarnation is going on?" she says, her voice shrill and agitated.

"Is that—" Tyrell's mom starts.

"We've got the situation under control," the first officer says. "My partner is securing the premises now."

The old woman stomps right up to the officer and wags her bony finger in her face. "That's my factory. I have a right to know what the devil is going on." Tyrell can see that the white dress isn't a wedding gown—more like a nightdress.

The officer straightens. "Well, Mrs. Schneider, we had a trespasser, and we caught him."

"It's *Miss. Miss* Schneider," Tyrell says quietly.

The old woman's face crinkles into an obliging smile. "Miss Schneider is correct. Been my name since 1922. Now, who broke in and why?"

Mom looks to Tyrell to respond, and the officer's pen stops.

"I did, ma'am," Tyrell says. "But I didn't really break in. I had a key."

"By yourself? Why go in there?" Miss Schneider leans forward, her wrinkled face inches from Tyrell's.

"Because I thought I saw someone up there who . . . needed help."

"Well, isn't that peculiar?" Miss Schneider says. "Why did you think that?"

"I saw a light," Tyrell explains.

"What in the world is going on?" His mom shakes her head and shivers.

"Would you like to press charges, Miss Schneider?" the officer asks.

The other officer emerges from the factory, dusting himself off. He closes the padlock and brings the key to Miss Schneider. "All clear up there," he says.

Miss Schneider takes the key and then studies Tyrell's face with her piercing, pale blue eyes. "What say I talk to the boy first?" She motions to her mansion. "Can I call you in an hour or two if I decide to press charges?" She totters slightly in her furry white slippers as she turns to face the officers.

"But I didn't do anything." Tyrell's heart thumps. *Would she really make me go with her? Am I going to be charged with trespassing if I don't—or maybe even if I do?*

"You're lucky all of this commotion didn't wake Dad," his mom says. "This would just about kill him, you breaking and entering."

"I didn't break in, I just entered!" Tyrell counters. "Because of the light."

"Because of the light," Miss Schneider echoes.

The officer pulls a business card from her front pocket. "Here's my contact information. My shift ends at six in the morning, so call before then and we can get this all settled." She hands the card to Miss Schneider.

"Come along, then," Miss Schneider says and motions for Tyrell to follow her back to the mansion.

His mom shrugs, raising her eyebrows and motioning for him to go. "I'm heading to bed," she says. "Hopefully Dad's still asleep." She storms back up the lane to their cottage.

Except for a light at the end of a dark hallway, the Schneider mansion is dark inside. Tyrell follows Miss Schneider down the passage to a warmly lit room.

A lamp with a deep red silk shade and long, silky tassels sits on a small, round, wooden table between two high-backed, burgundy velvet chairs. The yellow satin curtains are drawn tight.

Tyrell's heart thuds. *No one can see inside. And no one can hear me if I scream.. . . . Okay, maybe that's overdramatic.* They walk over a black-and-white marble floor and step onto a rich but worn rug. She motions for him to sit down in the chair to the left. A low fire crackles in a massive pink tile fireplace. A sleek black cat meows and jumps into Miss Schneider's lap just as she eases down into the other chair. *At least there is a phone on the table, though it's probably older than I am.*

"Now," Miss Schneider says as her wrinkled hands pat the arms of the chair. "Tell me what happened." She sets the officer's business card on the table.

Shadows dance on the walls. Above the fireplace hangs a huge painted portrait of a young woman bedecked with jewels and dressed in a flowing peach gown. Tyrell's eyes flit from the portrait to Miss Schneider.

"Is that you?" He nods to the portrait.

"Yes. Many years ago. It was painted a week before my wedding."

"But I thought—"

"It was the very day Leroy was shot. I was sitting for the painter while he lay dying in the woods." She looks down and strokes the cat. "I knew I'd never find another Leroy. And I wouldn't settle for second best." Her pale blue eyes fix on Tyrell's. "But I digress. You're here not to hear my stories but to explain why you broke into my factory."

Tyrell clears his throat. A shiver, like a prickly electric charge, runs through his chest and arms. She probably won't believe him. "Like I said, it was the light."

"The light?"

"Yeah. I was in the attic—you know, the cottages up there? My parents are remodeling one of them." He motions out the big picture window. "And I saw a light sending the S.O.S. code: three short flashes, three long, and then three short. I saw it two nights in a row."

"Why didn't you simply alert the authorities?"

"Well, what if it was just an electrical short? I mean, I'd feel totally stupid then."

"Indeed. So you saw this flashing and you went to investigate."

"That's right."

"And what, pray tell, did you find?" Miss Schneider's eyes widen. The cat stares at him from her lap.

He shakes the young girl's image from his mind. Miss Schneider will probably think he's using the madwoman tale to get out of trouble.

"Well?" Miss Schneider presses.

"A girl!" he says finally. "There was a girl up there."

Miss Schneider slowly nods. The cat closes its yellow eyes.

"And what did this girl look like?"

He shuts his eyes and pictures her. "She had on a white shirt and a long skirt. And her hair was up in this poofy bun thing."

"Ahh." Slowly Miss Schneider rises from the chair.

"You don't believe me." He looks at his hands. He's been gripping his knees so hard his knuckles are white.

"What was she doing?"

He shudders at the memory of the image in the window. "Sewing, maybe? There were flames."

"I never believed she had found work in the city," Miss Schneider says as she walks slowly to the far wall. "But I was just a little girl, what did I know?" She stops at a small desk and opens the front. "No one believed me. I saw the light flashing that night—I told Papa later, but he dismissed me." She pulls a small piece of paper from the desk. "What else did you see?"

"The flames . . . And a man."

"A man?" She walks slowly back to her chair, carrying a black-and-white photograph.

"Yes. He looked familiar."

Her head jerks to look at him. "Familiar? How so?"

"The article!" That's where he'd seen that face before. "I'm working on a paper about workers' rights, so I did research on Schneider Wearables. I saw his picture in a newspaper article about the new factory."

Miss Schneider hands him a yellowed photo of a girl.

"That's her!" Tyrell says. "Who is she?"

CHAPTER 10

A harsh north wind blasts the house, rattling the windows and sucking sparks up the chimney. Miss Schneider's head tilts, and the cat's black tail flicks as the glow of fire plays on her face, making her look young and then old. Miss Schneider holds the photo a few inches from her face.

"She played with me at the factory," she says. "I was born in 1922. My mother died of complications after my birth. My papa, Max Schneider, thrust himself into his work. He was always traveling, finding new sources of cotton and thread and the latest machinery."

"And Max—I mean, your papa, what was he like?"

"Dedicated. Punctual. Driven. He wanted to be successful." The cat paws around in her lap and lies down, purring.

The image of the man in the reflection forms in Tyrell's mind. He looked so angry, so insistent. And the girl had such a look of . . . fear—that's what it was—in her eyes.

"How driven?" Tyrell asks. "Did he have a temper?"

Miss Schneider turns abruptly to him. "He was driven. But fair. A bit of penny pincher, mind you. Now, if you want to talk about a temper we need to talk about the manager— oh, what was his name?" She raises her hand to her forehead. "That's it. Zinn. Mr. Zinn."

"A temper? What do you mean?" The wind blasts the window again. Tiny bits of ice clatter against the glass.

Miss Schneider grimaces and strokes the cat. "I had a dog, just a pup, and one time it jumped up on Mr. Zinn. That man kneed it so hard in the chest the dog collapsed. I asked him why, and he said he said he didn't want paw prints on his suit."

Some of the words from the letter come back to Tyrell: Ms. L said they meant "the boss is mean." He clears his throat. "So, your papa, he worked the workers hard?"

Miss Schneider folds her hands on her lap. "There were quotas, yes. The company made a lot of money. It was efficient."

"And he spoke German?"

"Yes. He could communicate with the workers. They liked him."

"And Mr. Zinn?"

"Mr. Zinn spoke only English. I remember she told me he was always yelling at them in English. 'Hurry, hurry,' he'd say."

"What happened to him?"

"Oh, after they moved to the new factory Mr. Zinn and Papa parted ways."

The girl, the letter, the keys, Mr. Schneider, Mr. Zinn—somehow they were all connected. "So your papa ran a sweatshop?"

"Not my papa." Miss Schneider raises an eyebrow and her voice grows stern. "He hired quite a few recently arrived Germans, but to give them opportunity, like he had." Her eyes narrow. "It was *not* a sweatshop, young man. He paid them a fair wage." She raises a bony finger at him. "Papa was born in Germany and proud of it. He even hired a governess to speak German to me. But why are you so interested in all of this?"

"Because I think," Tyrell says, "that someone did die in that fire—it was that girl. Maybe your dad knows—I mean knew—something about it. Maybe he was . . . "

The cat screeches and darts off Miss Schneider's lap. "Papa? Involved in her death! That's preposterous. I will not have you trespassing and then defaming my papa!" She slams the photo onto the table.

"But there was a man. I saw his face . . . from the article . . . and the fire—your dad never reported the girl missing!"

Miss Schneider's gray hair shakes as her voice rises. "The nerve of you, insulting my papa." She snaps up the business card and then the phone and dials. "Hello? Yes, Officer, it is Miss Schneider. I've decided I would like to press charges." She glares at Tyrell. "Yes. Yes. I see. I understand. No breaking, no vandalism. I see. Community service sounds appropriate." She hangs up the phone, and her icy glare freezes on Tyrell. "Are you ready to tell the truth?" she asks.

Tyrell's mind races. "I am telling the truth! I saw the flashing light, and I saw someone. And I bet you've seen it too!" He pops up from the chair. "You believe me. You know that girl! She worked for your dad, and then something bad happened. And you know something about this. You're hiding something!"

Miss Schneider's face is taut, her eyes large and fearful, but she waves at him dismissively. "There won't be any need to look into this matter anyway. That building is coming down the day after tomorrow."

A wave of nausea rushes over him. Miss Schneider knew the girl, saw the signal, but for some reason she is trying to cover it all up.

CHAPTER 11

It is nearly two in the morning when Tyrell finally falls into bed. He sleeps deeply until just before dawn, when he doesn't quite wake up but isn't quite asleep either. Someone is in his room.

He tries to open his eyes, but he can't move. Through the slits in his eyes he watches the girl at the desk writing a letter.

"What?" he gasps, desperately trying to sit up and see her.

She turns to him. *"Der Ofen,"* she says.

With a sharp gasp he bolts up, throwing off the comforter. But his room is empty, the girl gone. Dust swirls in lazy rivulets in the stream of light from the window. He stands and walks to the desk. What is she trying to tell him?

Just before eleven that morning, he goes down the narrow stairway to the kitchen. His mom and dad are sitting at the table, coffee cups in hand. A platter with syrup and a single pancake sits in the middle of the table. His mom eyes his dad and then him, as if to say, *Don't talk about it now.*

"How did you sleep?" she asks, a sharp edge in her voice.

"Okay. I guess I overslept."

Dad sets down his coffee cup. "Not getting chilled again, are you?"

Tyrell does feel chilled, not to mention exhausted, but staying home with an angry mom doesn't sound like a good plan either. "I'm fine. I have to go in. I can't miss any more or . . . "

"Or you could fail," his mom says.

"Yeah, that." Tyrell pulls the last pancake from the plate and eats it.

*****

As he gets out of the car at Middleton High the wind picks up. It is sharp, like a slap in the face. His mom drives off, and he tucks his hands into the pockets of his sweats. His fingers wrap around a soft piece of paper: the crumpled ten-dollar bill. Yes! He has just enough time to buy a cinnamon roll in the cafeteria before next period.

"What's this?" the lunch lady asks as she takes the bill.

"Ten dollars, right?" he says. His mouth waters as he eyes the sweet, buttery cinnamon roll.

"This doesn't look right." She holds it up to the fluorescent light. "No, something isn't right with this." She hands it to him and takes back the plate with the roll.

"Wait, what?" Tyrell holds the bill out.

"See?" She pulls another ten-dollar bill from the register and holds it up.

He lifts his bill next to hers and studies them. He'd been so excited about the letter that he never really looked at it. The back of his bill is greener than the other, and it shows an old Model T car. He flips the bills over. The front of his bill is dark, the ink almost black, but the same Alexander Hamilton face appears in the oval in the middle. But underneath that on his bill it says *Will pay to the bearer on demand TEN DOLLARS.*

"See what I'm saying?" The lady plucks her bill back. "It's not right."

He glances at the date: *series of 1928.* The bill and the letter are both from the same year as the fire. He must get to Ms. L and find out what the letter says.

"Ty!" Ms. L says from her office when he walks in.

"Did you translate that letter?"

"What? Oh, yes. I printed it out for you." She pulls a sheet of printed paper from a stack on her desk and hands it to him, along with the letter. "The date is blurry, but it's nineteen something."

Dear Mother,

I have found work! Elsa, another girl, told me about a sewing job out west. I took trains and trains and then a boat and now I am here, at the Schneider Wearables Factory, near the town of Middleton. It is beautiful here, very green with trees and lakes, like Bavaria. I sew dresses. I am not very good with the machine because I always sewed by hand before. The boss is mean, and he yells at us in English, always to work faster. If we do not meet the goal, then we must come to the factory after dinner, sometimes until after midnight, and sew. I am slow, so I will have to stay tonight. It is cold and dark in the factory at night since the oven is off, and my fingers move slowly. But tonight I will bring a candle and I will sew faster. Elsa leaves tomorrow for another new job in the big city of Seattle. We girls all stay together in a small cottage. There are many of us, but since there is no heat here, it is good for warmth. I play with the young girl here. She is much like our little Marie. I am sending you this ten dollars, and I will send more. Worry not, Mother, I am well.

Love, Helga

"What happened to her?" Ms. L says when Tyrell sets down the letter.

"Something bad," he mumbles.

"Why do you say that?"

The girl at the desk and in the factory, it has to be her—Helga. "There was a fire in the factory," he says. "The paper said no one died, but I think someone did. I think it was Helga." He lifts the letter. "Do you have more copies of that fire article?"

"Sure." Ms. L goes to her computer and clicks a few keys. The printer hums as papers spit out. "This one?" She hands him the Schneider Factory fire article, and he scans it.

"Here." He points. "September fourteenth, that's the date of the fire and also the date of this letter."

"That's why you think this Helga died in that fire?"

"That and something else. I know it."

"Have you talked to anyone else about this?" Ms. L says.

"No. Well, I did mention it to Miss Schneider."

"You saw her! Why didn't you say something?"

"She's accusing me of trespassing. I think I'm gonna have to do community service."

"Trespassing?"

"I went to the factory, and she saw me somehow and called the police. If I go back I'll get arrested, and they're demolishing the factory tomorrow. Now we'll never find out what happened. Yeah. I'm screwed. And I probably have community service."

"Community service isn't that bad."

"You only say that because you don't have to do it."

"Maybe. By the way . . . " Ms. L turns. "Was she in her wedding gown?"

"It was a long white thing, but maybe it was a nightgown?"

*****

Tyrell can barely concentrate in chemistry while all of the puzzle pieces float through his mind and connect. *Helga is slow at sewing on the machine. It's very cold up there and her hands freeze, so she brings a candle. Something in that bin catches fire. But she doesn't leave. Why doesn't she open the window? Because of the bars. Why doesn't she run out? The door is locked. The scissors!*

"She was trying to get out!" Tyrell blurts.

"Excuse me?" his teacher says. They're supposed to be balancing equations.

"He locked her in! The keys! Who had the keys?" Helga wasn't reported missing because whoever had locked her in would get in trouble. He'd just read that after the Shirtwaist Fire, stricter employee safety laws were enacted to prevent such tragedies. So someone must have hidden the body. *But where? In that room? Or in the chest? It wasn't burned, so it was moved in there later, after the fire. That had to be it! If I can find that key, I can open the chest.*

"Tyrell—" the teacher starts, but then the bell rings and Tyrell bursts out into the hallway.

He has to get to Miss Schneider before it's too late.

CHAPTER 12

"What's on your agenda for tonight?" his mom asks later, while she's cooking dinner. She sounds suspicious. She lifts the lid off the pot on the stove, and steam rushes up. Three pork chops sizzle in a skillet.

Tyrell shifts and looks at the food on the stove. "I might head down to, um, do some more research on my civics paper around six." He waves in the general direction of the mansion. His mom would absolutely lose it if she knew Miss Schneider had decided to press charges against him. "I'm going to interview Miss Schneider."

"The old woman in the mansion?" his dad asks as he sits down at the table. "One of the nurses said she walks around that place in her wedding gown."

"I think it's a nightgown," Tyrell says.

"Interview?" his mom says and stabs the chop with a fork.

"Yeah. I'm hoping she'll tell me the history of the factory."

"Really?" Mom's voice is uncertain. "I thought we were all done with that."

"Nope. There's one more thing I need to look into." Tyrell puts on his jacket. The keys are still somewhere on the second floor. *Someone tried to hide them because they opened all of the factory locks, even the chest. One more piece of information and the whole story will come together.*

He puts the letter and the ten-dollar bill into his backpack. Then he walks down the lane to the mansion and presses the doorbell. Somewhere deep inside a gong sounds.

The door clicks and opens.

"You?" Miss Schneider says irritably.

"I know what happened." Tyrell lifts the ten-dollar bill and the yellowed letter.

Miss Schneider closes her eyes and makes a

face as if someone has fed her bitter poison. "If you intend to drag my father and the Schneider name through the mud, young man, I suggest you cease and desist."

"No, that's not my plan. But there is a mystery here, and I think you want to know what really happened to your friend Helga as much as I do."

Her mouth forms an O and her hands go to her face.

He steps forward. "So, can we sit?"

CHAPTER 13

Miss Schneider leads him to the red velvet chairs. They sit, and the black cat circles his chair, tail up, yellow eyes staring.

"Tell me, who was it that made the girls sew faster, meet a quota?"

She turns from him, wringing her hands as she says softly, "Papa had goals. He was driven."

"Your dad was there—at the factory— making the girls work faster. You said he was punctual and demanding."

She nods. "Yes. He went every day."

"And night. He was there at night too?"

Her pale blue eyes catch his. "No," she says slowly. "He was home at night. For dinner with me."

"Every night?"

"Most nights. When he wasn't traveling."

"And the night of the fire, he wasn't home?"

"That's true."

"So where was he?"

"He was in Seattle." Miss Schneider sounds certain. "He was so worried about the fire—and that it might spread to the mansion—that he came home as soon as he heard."

"And when did he get here?"

"The first train in the morning."

"Can you prove it?" Tyrell has to be sure.

"Am I on trial, young man?"

"No. But we are trying to solve a murder."

"He came home that morning. I am sure of it. He was in Seattle. There was an event. I imagine he signed some papers with the dates."

"The fire was on the fourteenth of September, 1928."

"I have the files. If there was a contract signed it will be there."

Tyrell believes her. It would have been impossible for Max Schneider to have been in Seattle that night and also have been in the factory in time to lock Helga in. That leaves only one suspect. But he has to be sure.

Tyrell pulls out the yellowed letter. "I found this." He hands it to her. "You speak German, right?"

"Yes. I can read it." Her eyes scan the yellowed letter and her mouth forms the German words as she silently reads. She takes a breath and closes her eyes, letting her hands and the letter fall to her lap.

"And what does it say? About Helga?" Tyrell asks.

"It says that the boss locked them in at night if they failed to meet their quotas. It says that"—she runs her finger along the dark script—"Helga . . . sewed slowly, and she didn't meet her quota."

"That's right. So that night she went up to do extra sewing and she brought a candle with her. She was locked in. The candle got knocked over and lit something on fire, a barrel of something."

Miss Schneider nods. "Rags. Those barrels were full of oil-soaked rags for the machinery.

Quite flammable."

"Helga tried to get out. She used the scissors to try to break through the door. But she couldn't. She burned to death in that room."

"I knew it," Miss Schneider says in a shaking voice. "I knew she wouldn't leave and not say good-bye." The cat bounds into her lap. "There, there, Leroy," she says, and his purring fills the room as she strokes him.

"That picture you have. It's her, Helga."

"Yes," Miss Schneider says softly. "She played with me. She said I was like her little sister."

"Marie."

Miss Schneider raises the letter to her chest. "Oh, dear Helga," she says. "But where . . . ?" She shakes her head at the thought.

"It was very hot, and it was a small room. The walls, the wood, it was all burned—didn't you see it?"

Miss Schneider shakes her head no. "The place was locked up. With the floor burned and the stairs ruined from water damage, it wasn't safe to go up there. After Mr. Zinn cleared the place out, no was allowed. And he had the only key to that room."

"Mr. Zinn had the key?"

"Yes. He was the manager."

Tyrell sits back. Zinn didn't start the fire, but he got back too late to save her. And he lied about it; he said no one died because he would have gone to jail for locking her in. "The keys were his."

"Papa would never have allowed such practices!" Miss Schneider cries. "I tried to tell him about the flashing light. Helga was sending us a signal."

"And she still is." Tyrell leans closer to her chair. "What do you think she wants?"

Miss Schneider looks at the letter. "She must have known you would help her." Her eyes shine with tears. "I think she wants to be remembered, for people to know what happened."

"But they won't now because you're tearing down the factory tomorrow."

"No!" Miss Schneider holds up a finger. "Not until we go back there and find out what she wants."

CHAPTER 14

It is just getting dark when Miss Schneider
hands Tyrell the key and he opens the padlock.
"So, are you still pressing charges?" Tyrell asks.

"Oh, that." Miss Schneider waves her hand.
"I never called the police."

"You were lying?" Tyrell tilts his head
at her.

"Well, I had to know if you were fibbing
about seeing the madwoman with the scissors."

"And now you know."

"Now I know," Miss Schneider echoes.

They turn on their flashlights, and he helps
her up the first staircase. He scours the second
floor. "Found them!" he says and lifts the iron
key ring from the dust.

"Oh, be careful," Miss Schneider says, holding the chair steady as he climbs over the file cabinet and onto the seat.

The third floor is dark, but a faint glow comes from the burned room. The warped door creaks as he pushes it open.

"Helga?" he calls out, balancing on the charred floor joist. "We're here to help you." He turns to the window. The girl appears in the reflection. She nods.

Tyrell walks carefully over to the chest and crouches. Slowly he lifts the barrel key to the padlock. The lock springs open. He tugs the top up until the lid opens.

Inside are a tattered book and a satin ribbon. The book's blue cover is worn and washed out with age. The gold title is in German. The ribbon is faded to a very pale pink. He flips through the book's pages. The same black-and-white photo of the girl that Miss Schneider has is wedged in between the pages. Helga sits with smaller girl—Miss Schneider?—on her lap. She appears to be reading her a book. Helga has a ribbon in her hair. She wears a white, high-collared shirt and a locket around her neck.

"What do you see?" Miss Schneider calls from below.

Tyrell tucks the picture back into the book. "The chest," he says. He carries the book and the ribbon back out and stops at the top of the mangled staircase.

"Did you find her? Helga?" Miss Schneider says, her hands clasped at her chest, her eyes gleaming.

"In a way, yes." Tyrell shines the beam of his flashlight on the book and the ribbon.

Miss Schneider gasps and nods. Her eyes narrow and then widen. "She always wore that ribbon—it was a gift from her mother."

He leans over and dangles the ribbon. Miss Schneider reaches up and gently takes it.

"And this," Tyrell says. He drops the book onto the chair seat. Miss Schneider's hand rests on the cover. "Fairy tales," she says. "Helga read me German fairy tales."

"That's what was in the chest. But it doesn't prove that Zinn knew she was in the factory that night." Was that what Helga had been telling him, to open the chest?

"What is the German word for 'chest'?" he asks.

"*Kiste*," Miss Schneider says.

That wasn't what Helga said. He scans the room, the empty tables and broken chairs, the old wood-burning stove.

What was it she said when she appeared in my room? That's it.

"She said, 'often,'" he says.

"Often?" Miss Schneider repeats and shakes her head. Then her eyes grow big. "No!" She raises her hands, and her pale eyes meet his. "It's *ofen*! It means 'oven' . . . she means the furnace!"

Tyrell spins. Of course! He hurries to the wood-burning stove. The metal handle sticks, and he yanks up, hard. The heavy iron door screeches and he shines the beam in.

"What's there?" Miss Schneider calls.

"I'm looking!" he says. Thick gray ash fills the bottom of the stove. He reaches in and lightly digs, sifting through the cinders until

his fingers touch something smooth and cool.
He pulls it out. It is an oval locket. He rubs it
with his thumb, and the initials *HM* appear.
*Mr. Zinn arrived too late to save her, so he burned
her body in the furnace to hide the evidence!*

CHAPTER 15

"The Shirtwaist Factory Fire of 1911 was a disaster that prompted new legislation and the organization of the workers," Tyrell says. He stands in the front of the class. "In fact, we had a tragedy right here in Middleton."

The class is rapt as he tells the story of how he and Miss Schneider pieced together from the newspaper accounts and memory how one Wearables worker was never accounted for.

"Helga Müller was a fifteen-year-old immigrant worker," Tyrell says. "But she was also a daughter, a sister . . . " His eyes stop on Miss Schneider. "And someone's friend."

She nods from the back of the classroom. He clicks through a computer slideshow of old pictures of the factory floor. "Like many other poor workers, she felt she had no choice but to work extra hours when the boss made her. Mr. Zinn, the manager, locked her in until she finished her daily quota. But there was a fire, and she couldn't get out. Because there were new laws against treating workers so poorly, Mr. Zinn covered up her death to escape murder charges. But he didn't count on someone missing a poor worker."

Tyrell plays a video interview with Miss Schneider. In it she is wearing a bright blue velour jacket, jeans, and a small gold locket. She recounts her memories of how the factory operated under the new rules. "My father treated the workers with respect," she says. "And Helga was a worker but also a friend."

Then Tyrell shows the contract that proves Mr. Schneider was in Seattle the night of the fire, leaving his manager, Mr. Zinn, to run the factory. "Mr. Zinn claimed, falsely, that Helga had quit and moved away. He felt that nobody would miss an immigrant girl and used his power to cover up how he broke the law,"

Tyrell says. "Abuse like this is how workers' rights legislation came about and why we still need to protect workers."

The class is quiet.

"But Helga is at peace now," Miss Schneider says, standing up. "In fact, we're going to make the property into a park: Helga Müller Park. We're putting in a big memorial to her. She isn't forgotten."

Several students clap.

"How did you figure out that she was missing?" a boisterous classmate calls.

Tyrell shifts from foot to foot. *Would they believe the truth?* He glances around the room and says, "I just followed a beacon."

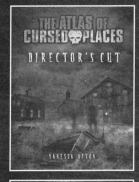

ABOUT THE AUTHOR

J. Fallenstein likes to freak herself out by constantly asking "what if?" She writes sometimes-scary stories that answer that question. You can find her at midnight in the Midwest wide awake wondering what that noise was.